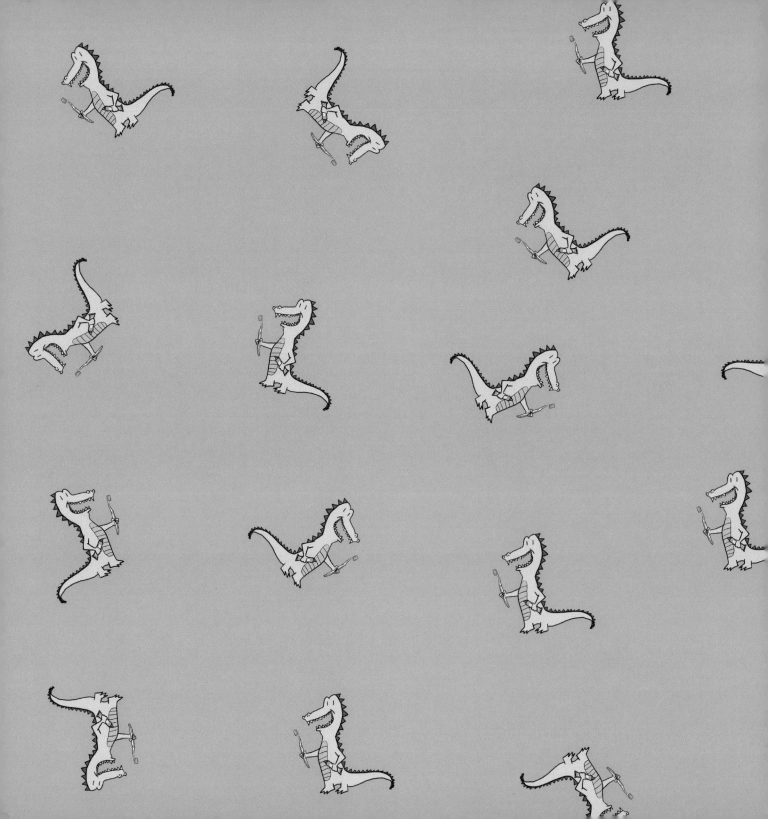

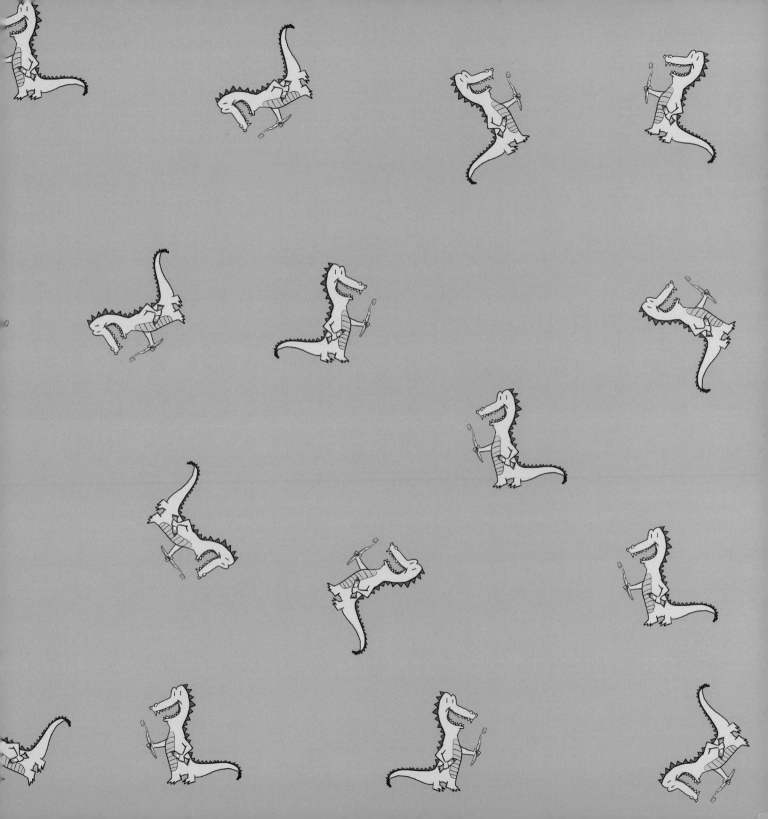

Dagobert goes to the dentist

Jean-Paul Colemonts

Dagobert is a very greedy crocodile. He loves candy, lollipops, muffins and all sorts of goodies. Dagobert really enjoys eating popcorn and watching tv in his free time.

One day, Dagobert had a terrible toothache and became very angry.

That dreadful toothache got worse and worse, so he had one of his splendid ideas.

Dagobert went to the dentist for the first time, and everything was new for him. Even though he was scared, he seemed to be very brave and sat in the dentist's chair.

The dentist put on his mask, got his dental mirror and started to examine Dagobert's big, big mouth.

Prevention is the best way to have excellent dental health. For good mouth hygiene, you should see your dentist twice a year and brush your teeth after every meal.

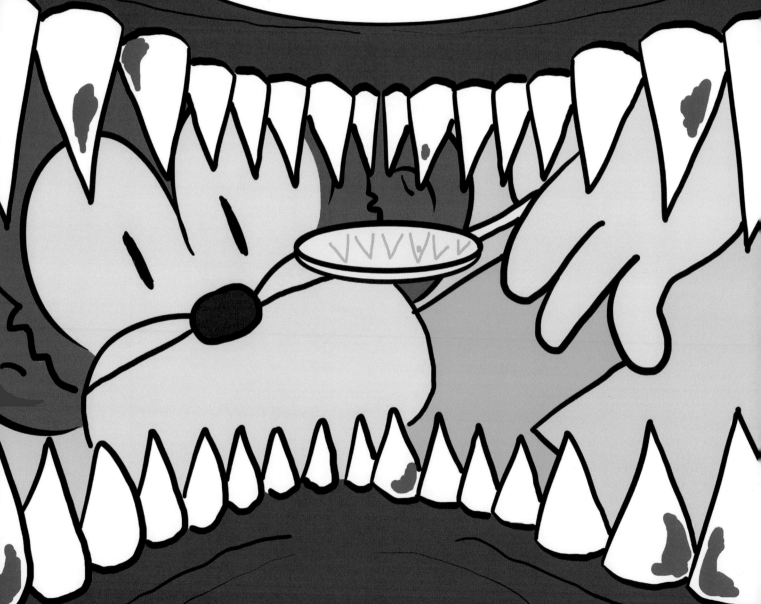

What have you been eating?
Well, I love to eat candy, lollipops, and chocolate and drink lots of soft drinks between my meals.

Water is a precious element for our well-being. More than 50% of the human body is composed of this valuable liquid. It's very important to keep our bodies hydrated, especially in the summer and when we do physical activities.

Let's help planet Earth.
Do not waste it.
Always turn the tap off
while you brush your teeth.

Dagobert had to go to the dentist once every week for a whole month because his teeth were badly decayed.

He learned that besides having balanced meals, brushing his teeth regularly helped to keep a lovely smile. He lives very happily nowadays.

The end.

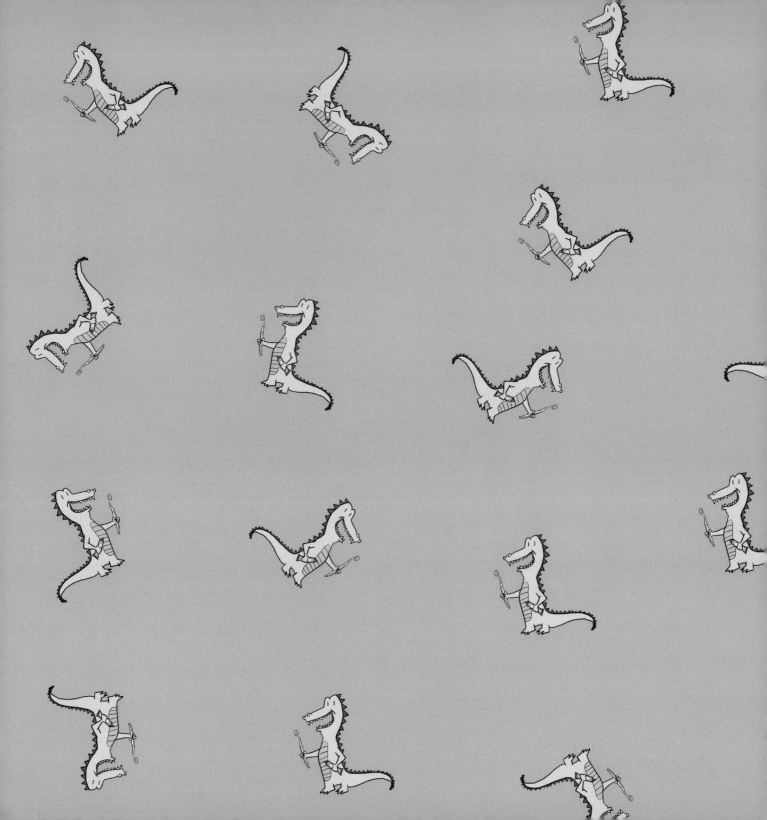

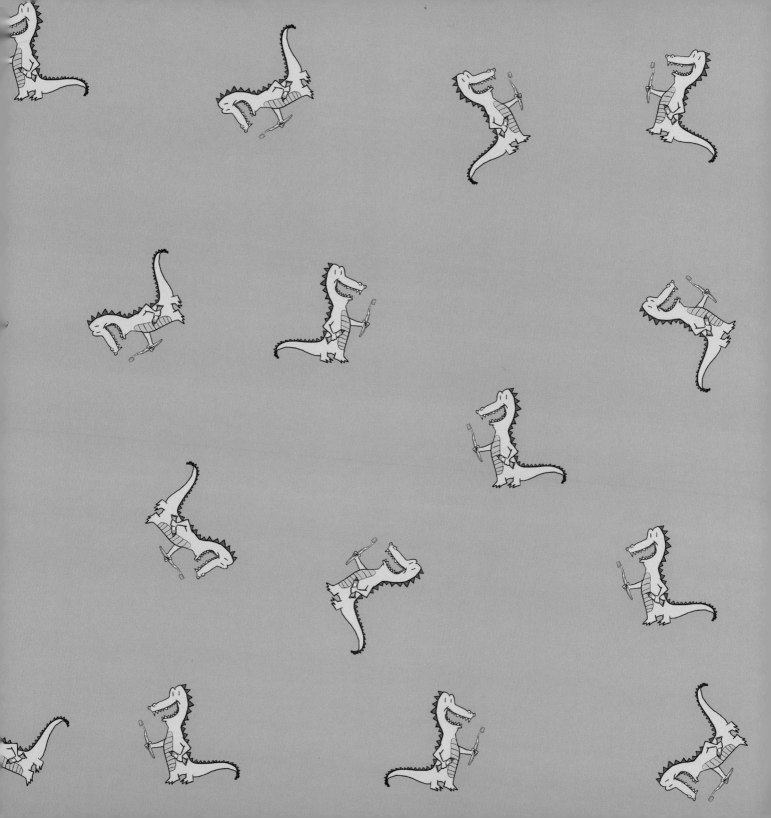